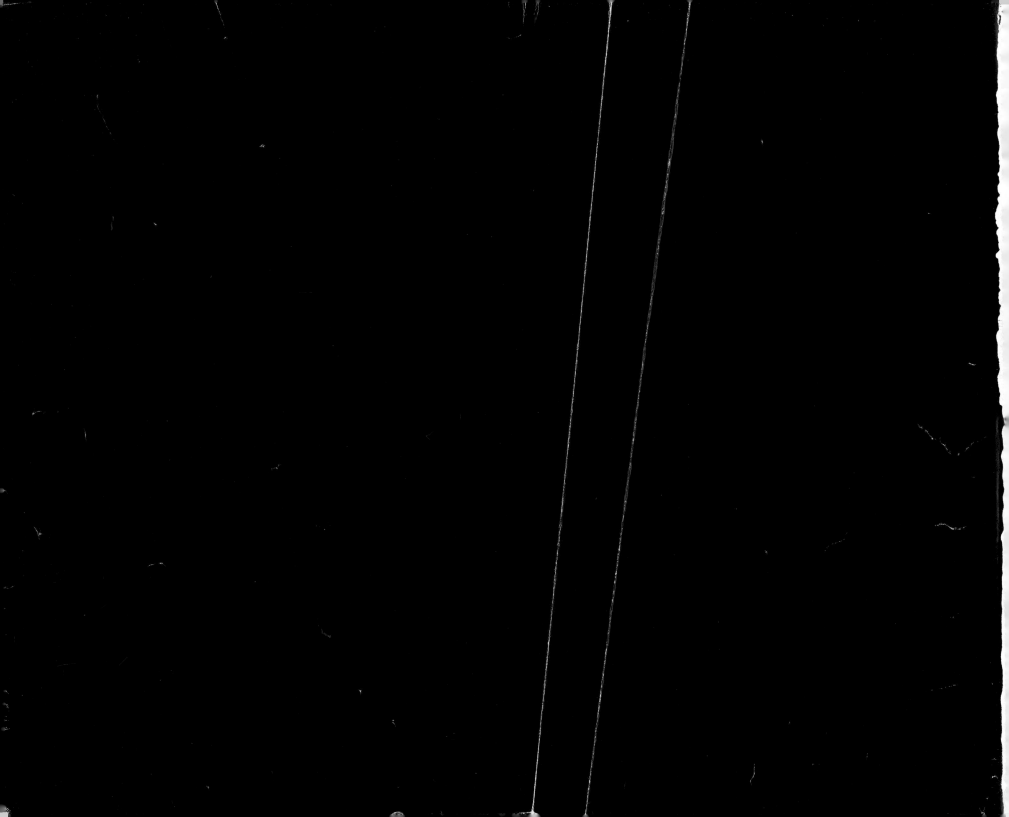

The Spooky Book

Steve Patschke

ILLUSTRATIONS BY Matthew McElligott

Walker & Company ☀ New York

You can ask any haunted house
or
bat flying kooky.
Is it true?
Yes it's true.
This book
is spooky!

To my sweethearts Grace, Katie, and little Zoë —S. P.

For Jessie and Christy —M. M.

Text copyright © 1999 Steve Patschke
Illustrations copyright © 1999 by Matthew McElligott

First published in the United States of America in 1999 by Walker Publishing Company, Inc.

Published simultaneously in Canada by Fitzhenry and Whiteside, Markham, Ontario L3R 4T8

Patschke, Steve.
The spooky book/written by Steve Patschke; pictures by Matthew McElligott.
p.   cm.
Summary: In a dark house, Andrew gets scared while reading a spooky book in which a girl
is reading a spooky book in a scary house.
ISBN 0-8027-8692-8 (hardcover). —ISBN 0-8027-8693-6 (reinforced)
[1. Fear Fiction. 2. Haunted houses Fiction. 3. Books and reading Fiction.]
I. McElligott, Matthew, ill. II. Title.
PZ7.P27567Sp 1999   99-13040
[E]—dc21   CIP

Book design by Sophie Ye Chin

Printed in Hong Kong
10 9 8 7 6 5 4 3 2

The house was dark.
One candle was lit.
Andrew shook
as he opened the cover
of a spooky book.
Thunder rumbled
far away
as Andrew gulped a fistful of popcorn.
Carefully he turned each dusty page.
And this is what
that spooky book
said . . .

Once there was a girl
alone
in a great big house.
Lightning cracked the sky,
and she shook
as she opened the cover
of a spooky
book.

"Same as me," whispered Andrew.

"She had no one to play with,
and she found a spooky book!
I wonder what her name is
or if she's frightened
or if she talks to herself
as much as I do?"
Andrew couldn't help
but read on.

The girl had fiery red hair and new sneakers.
Her name was Zo Zo.
"What's there to be afraid of?" Zo Zo asked herself.
"A book can't hurt you." Zo Zo began to read.
And this is what that spooky book said.

Once upon a time
in a great big house
haunted by ghosts and goblins,
a boy sat alone.
Slowly, outside the boy's window,
the wind began to howl
like a ghost. . . .

Suddenly,
the wind
outside Zo Zo's window
began to howl.

"It's a ghost!"

Zo Zo hollered,
and she jumped
to her feet
with a thud.

All of a sudden,
from outside Andrew's window,
there came a horrible howling.

"A ghost!"
Andrew cried,
and he jumped
behind the couch
with a thud.
But when he peeked out through the curtains,
he saw only branches blowing
in the wind.

"What's there to be afraid of?"
Andrew laughed.
"A book can't hurt you."
Reaching for more popcorn,
he read on.

As she turned the dusty page,
Zo Zo nervously twisted her hair.
She read about lightning
crashing and flashing and
shadows long and tall
that were just about to
CREEP,

CREEP,

CREEP

across a wall,

when suddenly . . .

lightning crashed and flashed, shadows
CREPT,
CREPT,
CREPT
across her wall.

"Goblins!"
Zo Zo cried, clutching her book.

"Goblins coming to get me!"
And out the front door poor

frightened Zo Zo

ran.

"I don't believe . . .
I don't believe . . .
I don't believe in goblins,"
Andrew shook.

Lightning lit up Andrew's wall.
"A goblin!" he cried out,
tossing his book
to the floor.

And you can ask any goblin
or
ghost walking droopy.
Is it true?
Yes it's true,
That book
was spooky!

Armed with a bicycle helmet
and a broom,
Andrew sneaked up to the wall.
But when he looked,
he saw only
a shadow.

"How could a spooky book do spooky things?"
whispered Andrew.

He hugged his favorite pillow
like a shield.
"I'm sure the redheaded
girl and I have
nothing to fear," he said.
Bravely, he opened his
book and read on.

Into the stormy night,
                    Zo Zo ran.
She ran very fast.
            "I don't believe in goblins. And
I don't believe in ghosts," she whispered.

The wind howled.

"Ghosts!" Zo Zo hollered.

Lightning flashed.

"Goblins!" Zo Zo cried. And down the rainy road she ran, like a wet rat in new sneakers.

"Will she be all right?" Andrew asked himself.

"She'll be fine," Andrew answered.

"As long as she doesn't end up anywhere spooky."

Andrew turned, as quickly as he could,
to the next page.

Soon Zo Zo came to a spooky, dark house.
"I think I saw a light," she said.
      "Maybe someone there could help me."
Through the creaky gate
   and up the crooked porch
      she crept.
      In her soggy new sneakers
      she shook.
   "Maybe I should knock," she said.

"Go on, knock!" said Andrew,
peeking at the pages through his fingers.

"What could happen?"

Zo Zo knocked,
    and the old door echoed.
From inside the house
    there came a MONSTROUS CRASH
        and then a long, fearful howl. . . . .

BAM!

BAM!

BAM!

came a knock on Andrew's door.

Andrew jumped, still holding the book.
His knees rattled like chicken bones.
He tripped and crashed over a broomstick,
a pillow, and a bowl of popcorn.

"Oooouuuch," he howled.

Frightened—Andrew
S L O W L Y
opened the door . . .

At that moment
the rain mysteriously
stopped.
A bright moon
poked through the
misty clouds.
An autumn breeze
blew by.

"Hi," said the girl,
"my name is Zo Zo,
and I'm your new neighbor.
What's your name?"

But Andrew could only
stare.
Because what should he
see in the girl's
shivering hand,
but a book,
the very same book
he held so near.
And . . .

You can ask any full moon
or
mist moving fluky.
Is it true?
Yes it's true.
That book . . .

was

SPOOKY!